BEACH LANE BOOKS
An imprint of Simon & Schuster Children's Publishing Division
1230 Avenue of the Americas, New York, New York 10020
Copyright © 2016 by Arthur Howard
BEACH LANE BOOKS is a trademark of Simon & Schuster, Inc.
For information about special discounts for bulk purchases, please contact Simon & Schuster
Special Sales at 1-866-506-1949 or business@simonandschuster.com.
The Simon & Schuster Speakers Bureau can bring authors to your live event. For more information
or to book an event, contact the Simon & Schuster Speakers Bureau at 1-866-248-3049
or visit our website at www.simonspeakers.com.
Book design by Sonia Chaghatzbanian
The text for this book was hand lettered.
The illustrations for this book were rendered in watercolor.
Manufactured in China
0716 SCP
First Edition

OCT 13 2016

2 4 6 8 10 9 7 5 3 1
Library of Congress Cataloging-in-Publication Data
Names: Howard, Arthur, author, illustrator.
Title: My dream dog / Arthur Howard.
Description: First edition. | New York : Beach Lane Books, [2016] | Summary: "A young pet owner knows lots about his dog, from what makes him
growl to when he is dreaming. But what does his dog dream about?"— Provided by publisher.
Identifiers: LCCN 2015043374| ISBN 9781481458382 (hardback) | ISBN 9781481458399 (e-book)
Subjects: | CYAC: Dogs—Fiction. | Dreams—Fiction. | BISAC: JUVENILE FICTION / Animals / Pets. | JUVENILE FICTION / Animals / Dogs. |
JUVENILE FICTION / Social Issues / Friendship.
Classification: LCC PZ7.H8283 My 2016 | DDC [E]—dc23 LC record available at https://lccn.loc.gov/2015043374

for Cora Howard

Here's my dog, Scooter.
I know a lot about him.

Heidi
the
German
shepherd

And what
makes
him
growl.

any dog that
goes near one
of his bones

And every word

he understands.

I know this means
he's thirsty.

This means he's scared.

This means he wants to play.

This also means he wants to play.

This means he
wants to play
right after
he's finished
playing.

I know my dog, Scooter, so well, I can even tell when he's dreaming.

—erf

What I don't know is what he dreams about.

My mom says he dreams about food.

My dad says he dreams about riding in the car.

My brother says Scooter
dreams about chasing things.

My friend Franklin says Scooter dreams about going to school.

Julie Potts, the smartest girl in my class, says his dreams are filled with sounds we can't hear

and smells we can't smell
and it's always snowing
in his dreams because
dogs are really wolves...

and wolves love snow.

Then I asked Grandpa and he said,

"Maybe Scooter dreams about you."

I never thought of that.

But I know a lot about Scooter, and I think it might be true.